Isaac on the Farm

The Sound of Long I

by Cecilia Minden and Joanne Meier • illustrated by Bob Ostrom

The Child's World

Published by The Child's World®
1980 Lookout Drive
Mankato, MN 56003-1705
800-599-READ
www.childsworld.com

The Child's World®: Mary Berendes, Publishing Director
The Design Lab: Design and page production
Richard Carbajal: Color

Library of Congress Cataloging-in-Publication Data
Minden, Cecilia.
  Isaac on the farm : the sound of long i / by Cecilia
Minden and Joanne Meier ; illustrated by Bob Ostrom.
    p. cm.
  ISBN 978-1-60253-405-6 (library bound : alk. paper)
  I. Meier, Joanne D. II. Ostrom, Bob. III. Title.
PE1157.M566 2010
[E]—dc22   2010002917

Printed in the United States of America in Mankato, MN.
July 2010
F11538

NOTE TO PARENTS AND EDUCATORS:

The Child's World® has created this series with the goal of exposing children to engaging stories and illustrations that assist in phonics development. The books in the series will help children learn the relationships between the letters of written language and the individual sounds of spoken language. This contact helps children learn to use these relationships to read and write words.

The books in this series follow a similar format. An introductory page, to be read by an adult, introduces the child to the phonics feature, or sound, that will be highlighted in the book. Read this page to the child, stressing the phonic feature. Help the student learn how to form the sound with her mouth. The story and engaging illustrations follow the introduction. At the end of the story, word lists categorize the feature words into their phonic elements.

Each book in this series has been carefully written to meet specific readability requirements. Close attention has been paid to elements such as word count, sentence length, and vocabulary. Readability formulas measure the ease with which the text can be read and understood. Each book in this series has been analyzed using the Spache readability formula.

Reading research suggests that systematic phonics instruction can greatly improve students' word recognition, spelling, and comprehension skills. This series assists in the teaching of phonics by providing students with important opportunities to apply their knowledge of phonics as they read words, sentences, and text.

The letter i makes two sounds.

The short sound of **i** sounds like **i** as in: *itch* and *ditch*.

The long sound of **i** sounds like **i** as in: *bike* and *ripe.*

In this book, you will read words that have the long **i** sound as in: *mile, wide, tires,* and *pie.*

Isaac is visiting Grandfather and Grandmother.

They live on a farm.

Isaac likes to do many things on the farm.

Isaac likes to climb trees.

He can see for miles.

He sees the wide river.

He sees the white clouds.

Isaac rides on a tractor.

The tractor has big tires.

Isaac sits beside Grandfather.

They ride across the fields.

Isaac helps Grandmother make five pies. The pies are for the fair. "I hope you win first prize, Grandmother!"

Grandmother gives Isaac some pie. Isaac takes a big bite. "This is nice!"

Here comes Ira. He lives next door. "Let's play a game," says Isaac. "We will hide in the barn."

What a good idea! They play all day. They have a good time on the farm.

Fun Facts

Fruit pies are a popular dessert in the United States and have been since colonial times. People traditionally eat pumpkin pie at Thanksgiving. Many people consider baking apple pies to be an American cooking tradition. But not everyone likes fruit in their pie. In Europe, people have been eating meat pies since the Middle Ages. Instead of cherries or pecans, some Europeans prefer their pies to be filled with steak, pork, fish, chicken, or other meats.

Maybe you've received a prize for winning a spelling bee or a relay race. Perhaps one day you'll go on to win a famous prize such as the Nobel Prize. The Nobel Prize is awarded to people who have made great contributions to science, literature, economics, or peace. This famous prize was first awarded in 1901. It is named for the Swedish inventor Alfred Nobel.

Activity

Organizing a Pie Baking Contest

Talk to your friends and their families about having a pie-baking contest. Set a date, and arrange for each family to bring a different pie. Everyone should try a little piece of each pie and then vote on which one tastes the best.

To Learn More

Books
About the Sound of Long I
Moncure, Jane Belk. *My "i" Sound Box®*. Mankato, MN: The Child's World, 2009.

About Pie
Munsch, Robert N., and Michael Martchenko (illustrator). *More Pies!* New York: Scholastic, 2003.
Priceman, Marjorie. *How to Make an Apple Pie and See the World*. New York: Knopf, 1994.
Thompson, Lauren, and Jonathan Bean (illustrator). *The Apple Pie That Papa Baked*. New York: Simon & Schuster Books for Young Readers, 2007.

About Prizes
Capucilli, Alyssa Satin, and Pat Schories (illustrator). *Biscuit Wins a Prize*. New York: HarperCollins, 2004.
Pin, Isabel, and Nancy Seitz. *When I Grow Up, I Will Win the Nobel Peace Prize*. New York: Farrar, Straus and Giroux, 2006.
Sharmat, Marjorie Weinman, and Marc Simont (illustrator). *Nate the Great and the Fishy Prize*. New York: Coward-McCann, 1985.

Web Sites
Visit our home page for lots of links about the Sound of Long I:
childsworld.com/links

Note to Parents, Teachers, and Librarians: We routinely check our Web links to make sure they're safe, active sites—so encourage your readers to check them out!

Long I
Feature Words

Proper Names
Ira   Isaac

Feature Words with the
Consonant-Vowel-Silent E
Pattern
beside   nice
bite   ride
five   time
hide   tire
like   white
mile   wide

Feature Words with Other
Long Vowel Pattern
climb   pie
idea

Feature Words with Blend
prize

About the Authors

Cecilia Minden, PhD, is the former director of the Language and Literacy Program at the Harvard Graduate School of Education. She is now a reading consultant for school and library publications. She earned her PhD in reading education from the University of Virginia. Cecilia and her husband, Dave Cupp, live outside Chapel Hill, North Carolina. They enjoy sharing their love of reading with their grandchildren, Chelsea and Qadir.

Joanne Meier, PhD, has worked as an elementary school teacher, university professor, and researcher. She earned her BA in early childhood education from the University of South Carolina, and her MEd and PhD in education from the University of Virginia. She currently works as a literacy consultant for schools and private organizations. Joanne lives in Virginia with her husband Eric, daughters Kella and Erin, two cats, and a gerbil.

About the Illustrator

Bob Ostrom has been illustrating children's books for nearly twenty years. A graduate of the New England School of Art & Design at Suffolk University, Bob has worked for such companies as Disney, Nickelodeon, and Cartoon Network. He lives in North Carolina with his wife Melissa and three children, Will, Charlie, and Mae.